MY MORNING SOUNDS

by Shawndre Johnson

Illustrated by Roger James

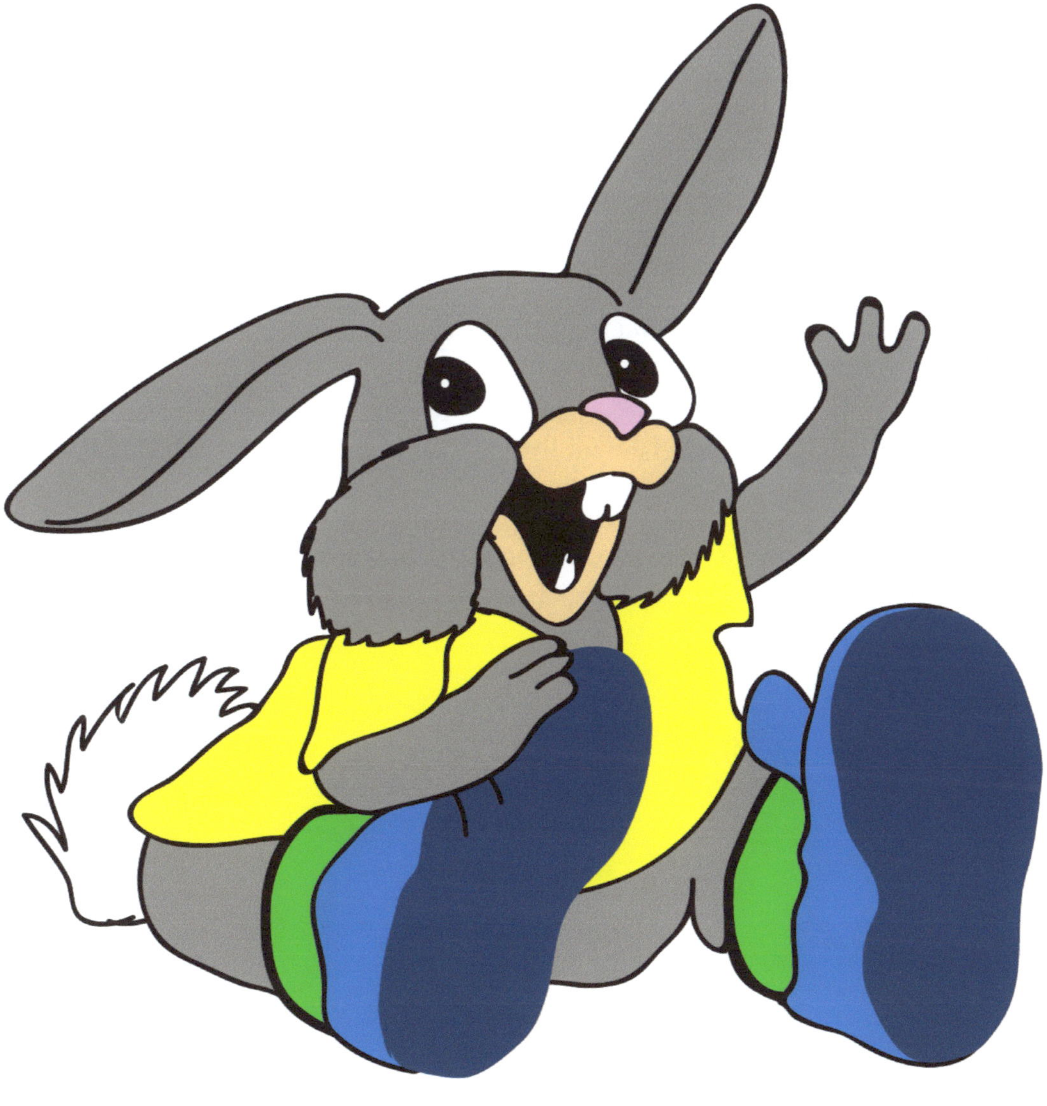

This book is dedicated to every child and parent who has helped me to
understand more along my journey to becoming a better therapist.
- Shawndre Johnson

Book Published By:
Nelson Publishing, LLC
Bowie, Maryland 20718
www.nelsonpublishingbooks.com

ISBN-13: 978-1-7335604-1-2
eBook ISBN- 13: 978-1-7335604-0-5

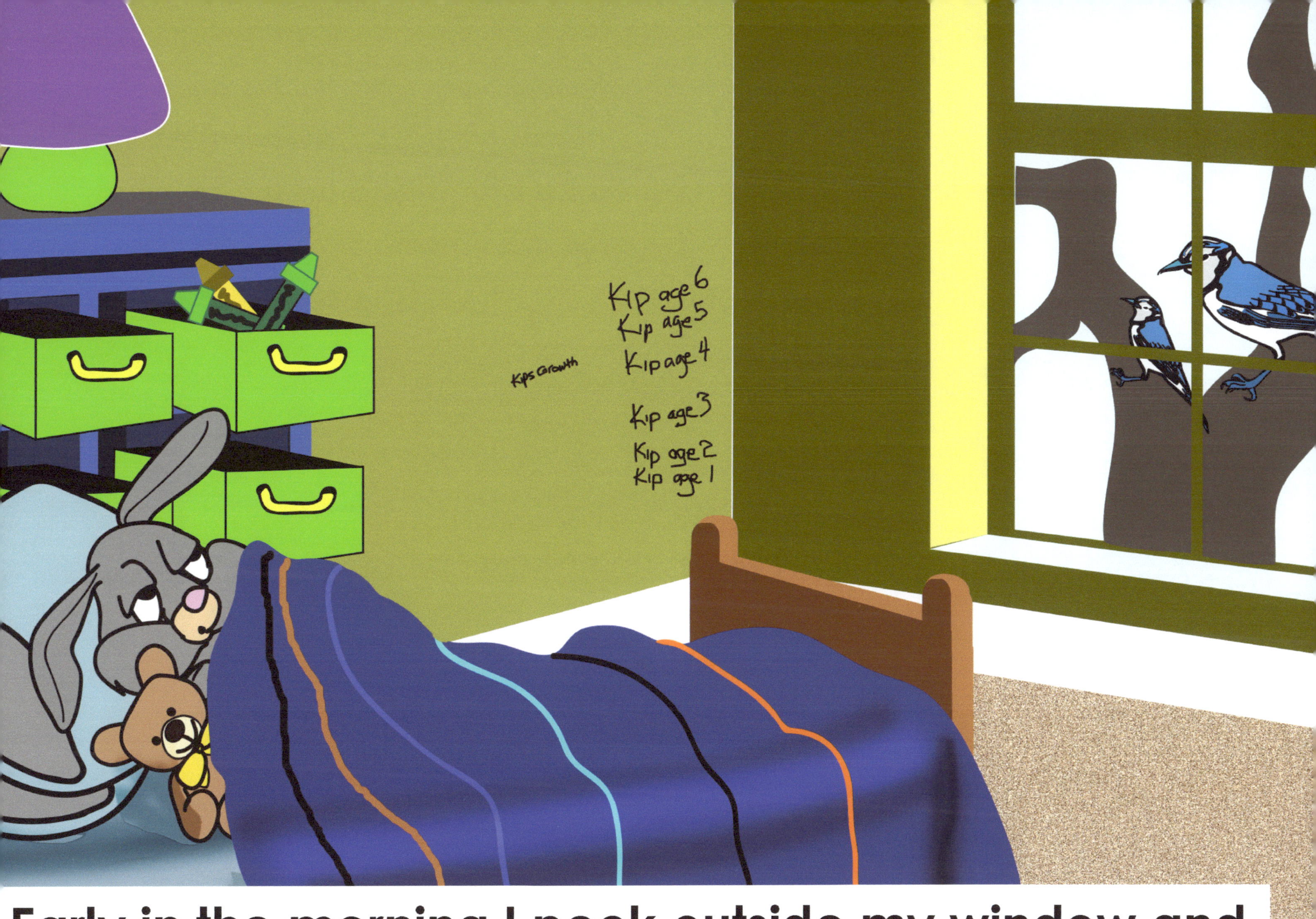

Early in the morning, I peek outside my window and see the sun rising. I watch the sun go up, up, up, up.

Stop. Listen. Quietly, the clock is ticking. Can you hear the sound? Tick, tock, tick, tock.

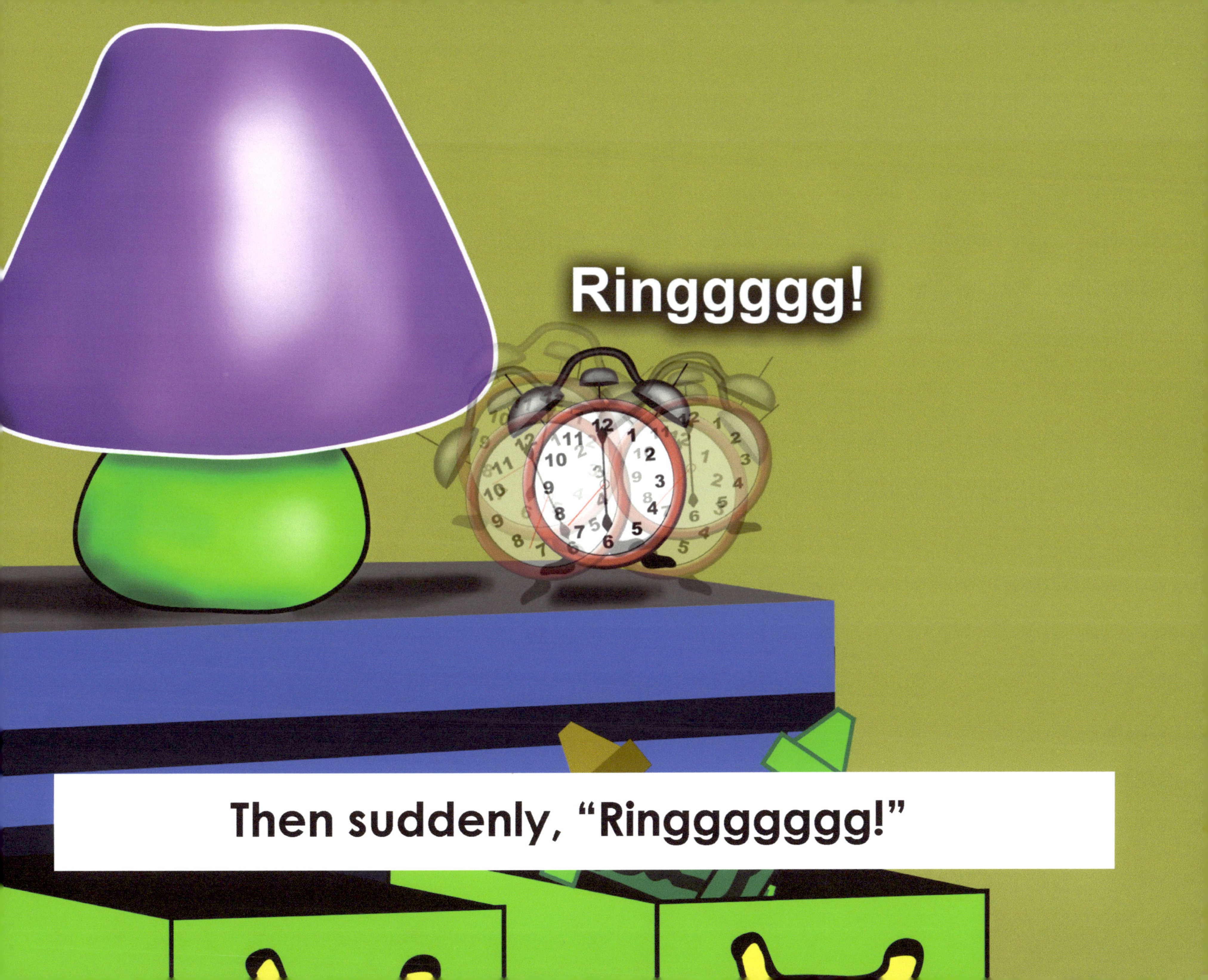

Then suddenly, "Ringgggggg!"

"Kip!" Mom calls. "It's time to get ready for school today."

It's time to start my morning sounds!"
Kip age 4
Kip age 3
Kip age 2
Kip age 1
"Time to start my morning sounds!" Kip shouts.

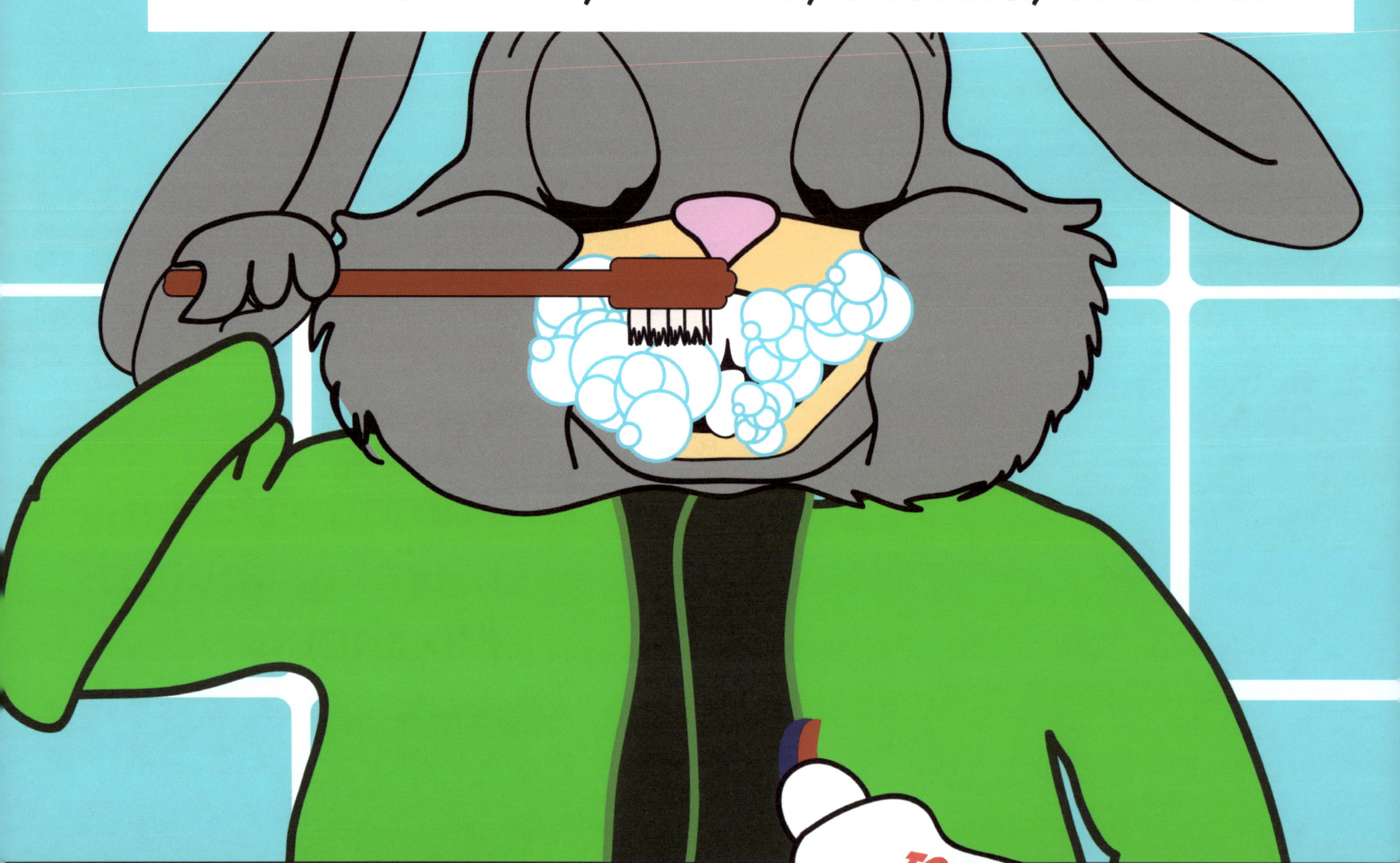

Quick! Hop out of bed and dash in the bathroom to brush my teeth. I go up and down with my toothbrush. Can you hear the sound? Chukka, chukka, chukka, chukka.

SOAP
Reach for the soap to wash my face. I like to make circles with my washcloth. Can you hear the sound?   Wipe, wipe, wipe, woooosh.

Pull on my pants and slip on my shirt. I put them on all by myself. Can you hear the sound? Whip, whip, whoop, whoop.

Tug on green socks and slide on blue shoes. I wiggle my toes inside. Can you hear the sound? Shum, shum, shoop, shoop.

"Kip!" Mom calls. "It's time to eat your breakfast."

un down to the kitchen to eat my breakfast. Wait! Slow down. y not to slip. Can you hear the sound? Stomp, stomp, stomp, go!

Sit at the table to eat pancakes and bacon. I stuff my mouth with my favorite breakfast. Can you hear the sound? Munch, mmmm, mmmm, yummy.

Drink a glass of ice cold milk. I stir in some chocolate to make it just right. Can you hear the sound? Gulp, gulp, gulp, aaaaah!

Grab a warm coat and a fuzzy hat. I can put them on, so mommy doesn't have to help. Can you hear the sound? Z-Z-Zip oooooh!

Bumpity Bump! Here comes the bus with all my friends. I listen for the horn. Can you hear the sound? Beep, beep, beep, beep.

"Kip, here's your backpack!" Mom calls.

Give a big hug to mommy. I know she will be here when I get back. Can you hear the sound? Kiss, kiss, kiss, squeeze.

"Morning sounds started your day. Now you're off to school to play! Good-bye, Kip."

3
4
5

"My morning sounds are done and my sounds at school will be just as much fun."

EMERGENCY OUT
STOP ON RED SIGNAL
"Bye-bye, mommy."

TARGET VOCABULARY

clock slippers  bathroom 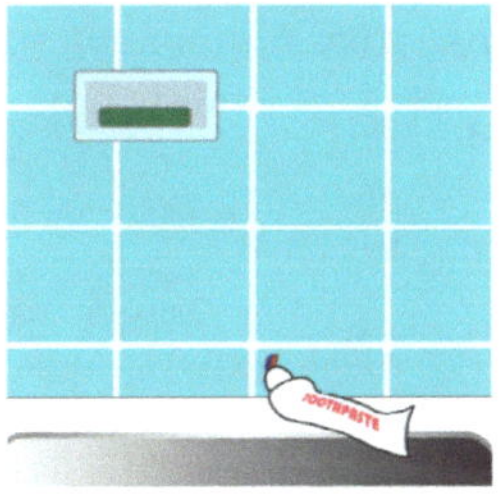 toothbrush  washcloth  shirt  pants

socks  shoes  kitchen  hat  coat  backpack 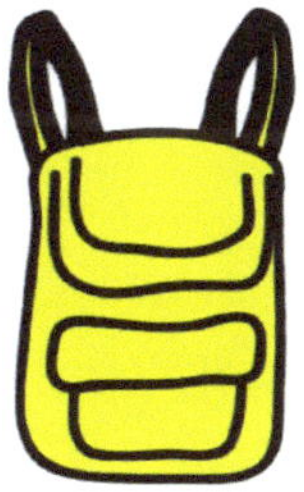 bus

Talking with Books: Tips for Parents

Reading to your child is one of the best ways to increase his or her speech and language and early literacy skills. As you read this book you will have opportunities to support your child's speech and language by working on skills such as imitating actions, making speech sounds, learning vocabulary, and answering questions. Practicing these skills supports oral language development which lays the foundation for reading instruction that will happen in your child's classroom. Feel free to read the book straight through while your child sits and listens to the story. You may also follow the suggestions below:

BEFORE READING

1. Start by finding a cozy place to read with your child. Add a blanket, a lamp, or a favorite pillow or stuffed animal so that it is a comfortable area for you and your child. If possible, establish this as your "reading corner" to use each day. This helps to make reading a special part of your daily routine.

2. Reading instruction begins with the cover of the book. Point to the words in the title and the names of the author and illustrator as you read the cover of the book. This works on increasing your child's awareness of print. For your preschool or kindergarten child, explain that the author is the person who writes the story and the illustrator is the person who draws the pictures.

3. Use the picture on the cover to work on prediction skills. This builds critical thinking. Ask your child questions like, "Where do you think the bunny is going?" or "What do you think the bunny is going to do?" and see if he or she can make a prediction.

4. Use words like 'think' or 'wonder' as you make predictions. Model statements that try to predict what will happen in the story. You can use sentences like, "I wonder if the bunny is going to walk to school or ride the bus to school" or "I think the bunny will ride the school in mommy's car".

DURING READING

1. Use expression in your voice when reading to your child. Change your volume and use different voices for each character to keep your child interested. For example, you can use a softer voice to read the repetitive line "Can you hear the sound?" to get your child ready to listen as you make the sound for each item.

2. Make the sound for the item and then tell your child, "It's your turn. You make the sound of the clock."

3.   Include movement so the story is more engaging for your child. Add movement to each sound by pairing the sound with an action. For example, make the sound of the toothbrush while pretending to brush your teeth. Encourage your child to do the action and make the sound as well.

4.   Talk about the pictures because books are more than just words. Ask your child to point to pictures of target vocabulary words ("Point to the clock" or "Can you find his slippers?"). This builds your child's understanding of labels for the pictures. After your child points to the slippers, you can model that vocabulary word in a sentence. Examples are: "Yes, those are Kip's slippers" or "You found his slippers under the bed."

5.   Make comments about the pictures and describe the actions in the pictures. Example: "Kip has a teddy bear. I bet his teddy bear feels soft and cuddly." You could also say, "Kip is brushing his teeth. He put toothpaste on his toothbrush." Encourage your child to tell you something about the pictures.

6.   Ask your child questions about what Kip is doing and what is happening in the book. Example: When Kip is in the bathroom, ask, "What is he doing with the wash cloth?" This gives your child a chance to use action words like wiping, sleeping, drinking, or brushing throughout the story.

7.   Ask "where" questions to help your child use location words like 'in', 'under', or 'behind'. Example: "Where are Kip's toys?" or "Where are Kip's slippers?" or "Where is he eating breakfast?"

8.   Talk about ways that the book connects to your daily life. Example: "Kip sleeps with a teddy bear just like you do" or "His clock goes off just like mine does early in the morning. My clock is noisy when it wakes me up."

AFTER READING

1.   Ask questions about what Kip did in the story. This gets your child using nouns and action words from the story. Example: "What did Kip eat for breakfast?" or "What did Kip do with the washcloth?" or "Who does Kip hug before he leaves for school?"

2.   Tell your child your favorite part of the story. Example: "I liked when Kip drank the chocolate milk because I love chocolate milk, too! That was my favorite part of the story". Ask your child what part of the story he or she liked the most.

3.   Do a follow-up activity that relates to the story like making pancakes or chocolate milk with your child. Another example could be to draw pictures of something Kip did in the story. You can also role play with your child by pretending to ride the bus like Kip. One person can be the driver and the other person can pretend to be Kip. Talk about things you might see on the ride to school.

4.   Refer back to the story as you go through daily activities. For example, when you are getting dressed the next day, refer back to Kip getting dressed in the story. Example: You can say, "Kip put on his shoes to go to school. They had carrots on them." Then, you can ask your child to tell you what is on his or her own shoes.

Now you have several strategies for interacting with your child as a part of your daily reading routine and you can be creative with your own ideas as well. Using these strategies is a great way to support expansion of your child's language and literacy skills. Most importantly, the fun and excitement that you convey to your child while reading sets the stage for a lifetime love of reading and learning. Enjoy reading with your child and keep talking with books!

About The Author

Shawndre Johnson, M.S., CCC-SLP, is a Speech-Language Pathologist with a love for helping children and families. She has achieved awards for continuing education from the American Speech-Language Hearing Association and has provided therapy services in public and private settings for over 22 years, including the highly recognized Kennedy Krieger Institute in Baltimore, Md. The bulk of her career has focused on serving the early childhood population where developing strong oral language and literacy skills is critical for preparing little ones with a strong start on their journeys to become good communicators and readers. Currently, she is focused on writing books that will provide parents with a fun and powerful way to reinforce speech and language skills at home.

Shawndre is a wife and mother who enjoys trying new foods, reading, decorating, and learning to play the piano.